Scholastic's
The Magic School Bus
GETS BAKED IN A CAKE
A Book About Kitchen Chemistry

SCHOLASTIC INC.
New York Toronto London Auckland Sydney

Based on the episode from the animated TV series produced by Scholastic Productions, Inc. Based on *The Magic School Bus* book series written by Joanna Cole and illustrated by Bruce Degen.

TV tie-in book adaptation by Linda Beech and illustrated by Ted Enik.
TV script written by Brian Meehl, John May, and Jocelyn Stevenson.

ISBN 0-590-22295-3

Copyright © 1995 by Scholastic Inc.
All rights reserved. Published by Scholastic Inc.
SCHOLASTIC and THE MAGIC SCHOOL BUS
are registered trademarks of Scholastic Inc.

Library of Congress Cataloging-in-Publication Data

Beech, Linda.
Scholastic's The magic school bus gets baked in a cake : a book
about kitchen chemistry / based on the episode from the animated TV
series produced by Scholastic Productions, Inc. ; based on the Magic
school bus book series written by Joanna Cole and illustrated by
Bruce Degen.
p.   cm.
"TV tie-in book adaptation by Linda Beech and illustrated by Ted Enik;
TV script written by Brian Meehl, John May, and Jocelyn Stevenson"-
-T.p. verso.
ISBN 0-590-22295-3 :
1. Baking—Juvenile literature. 2. Cake—Juvenile literature.
[1. Baking. 2. Cake. 3. Degen, Bruce, ill.] I. Cole, Joanna.
II. Scholastic Productions. III. Title. IV. Title: Magic school
bus gets baked in a cake.
TX765.B417 1995
540—dc20
94-38834
CIP
AC

12 11 10 9 8   5 6 7 8 9/9 0/0
Printed in the U.S.A.   24
First Scholastic printing, February 1995

Our teacher, Ms. Frizzle, is always surprising us. So on her birthday, we decided to surprise her. We planned a big party. We had balloons, streamers, confetti, and even noisemakers.

"We thought of everything," said Carlos.

But Arnold wasn't so sure. "Something's missing," he said.

I wonder if they'll remember *my* birthday.

Dorothy Ann was the only one who was not getting ready for the party. She was finishing her chemistry experiment.

"What are you working on at a time like this?" asked Carlos.

Dorothy Ann explained, "I'm mixing three things together—water, sand, and cement—to make something new—concrete. That's chemistry!"

That's when Arnold shouted, "I know what's missing! A birthday cake!"

My mother once made a cake that was like concrete.

We decided to put away the party things for later. We were upset—what was a birthday party without a cake?

When Ms. Frizzle came in, she saw our sad faces. "I see you've heard the news," she said. "The bus is not working well, so we won't be able to go to the bakery. I think I have to cancel our chemistry field trip."

"Bakery? What does a bakery have to do with chemistry?" asked Ralphie.

A bakery! What a sweet idea!

"A bakery is a small chemical factory," said the Friz.

Dorothy Ann added, "Baking *is* chemistry because things are mixed together to make something new."

Suddenly, Carlos realized that a bakery did indeed make something new—cakes! "Oh, Ms. Frizzle," he said, "our education wouldn't be complete without a trip to *this* chemical factory."

"Maybe the bus can get us to the bakery," said Ms. Frizzle. "Class, it's time for a field trip!"

Somehow, the bus did get us there. But as soon as we arrived, the bus began hopping

and stretching

and then it shrank to the size of a toy car—with us in it!

"How will we ever get inside the bakery now?" asked Wanda.

This is no small problem.

Oh, yes it is! We're so small!

Ms. Frizzle wasn't worried. She pushed a button. Suddenly, the tiny bus sailed through the mail slot of the bakery door. Inside, we could see a baker and some customers.

While the bus zoomed around the bakery, we took a good look at the cakes. Not one was chocolate!

"What will we do?" whispered Arnold. "The Friz likes chocolate."

Carlos thought hard. "We'll bake a cake," he said.

Hmmm. It could be the shrinker-scope or the mesmerglobber!

"It will be *our* chemistry experiment!" said Dorothy Ann.

"How will we get Ms. Frizzle out of the bakery?" asked Wanda. "We don't want her to see what we're doing."

Carlos remembered an auto parts store next to the bakery. He told the Friz that it might have the parts she needed to fix the bus. Ms. Frizzle thanked him, put on her jet pack, and took off. She left Liz in charge.

That baker is bugging me.

By this time, the bus was the size of a moth. When the baker saw it flying around, he became angry. He got his flyswatter and chased us into the kitchen. Finally, Liz set the bus down behind some jars. The baker couldn't see us.

Luckily, some customers came into the shop, so the baker left us alone.

"Come on!" said Carlos. "We've got work to do." He began to read a cookbook. "First we have to gather and measure the ingredients."

Everyone had a job. Ralphie got two eggs. But one egg got away from him. Wanda and Tim got the flour and sugar. Liz found a way to measure the salt and cream of tartar.

Arnold had some trouble carrying the baking soda. First he bumped into Dorothy Ann. Then he knocked over a bottle of vinegar. When the baking soda spilled on the vinegar, there was quite a reaction.

Keesha poured the milk, while Phoebe somehow got the butter. And Ralphie finally caught the runaway egg at "eggs-actly" the right moment.

Just then, Ms. Frizzle came back. Dorothy Ann thought fast. She had to keep the Friz away from the cake we were baking.

"Ms. Frizzle, could you help me with a chemistry experiment?" she asked. They began to experiment with the vinegar and baking soda.

The rest of us struggled with the measuring. The ingredients were bigger than we were!

"This is hard when you're half the size of a hot dog," complained Arnold.

"It could be worse," Ralphie told him.

Suddenly, it was. The bus rattled and shook. Then it shrank again—and so did we. Even tiny grains of salt and sugar looked like building blocks and diamonds.

"Let's go!" called Carlos. "We've got to make this cake before the baker catches us."

He was right. So we hopped on the bus and whipped into action. Last of all, we added the best and most delicious ingredient, the chocolate.

You might say the bus did all the work.

But the baker was our problem. When he saw the bus in action, he thought it was the moth again. So, he called the bug control company. For some reason, no one there believed that a moth could bake a cake.

You'd think he owned the place!

Meanwhile, Dorothy Ann and Ms. Frizzle were still doing chemistry experiments. When the Friz wanted to find the rest of us, Dorothy Ann had to stop her.

"What would happen if I put a whole bunch of baking soda into a bottle with the vinegar?" she asked.

The Friz loved the idea. "There's only one way to find out," she said.

So Dorothy Ann filled the bottle. The mixture fizzed over. It was a gas! Then Dorothy Ann put a balloon over the top of the bottle. The gas pushed out the sides of the balloon. The balloon got bigger and bigger.

Dorothy Ann's getting a rise out of this.

"Just like a tire filling with air," said Dorothy Ann.

That reminded Ms. Frizzle of the bus. "The bus needs new tires," she said.

As the Friz blasted off to check the bus tires, Dorothy Ann's balloon popped. Everyone cheered, though, because Ms. Frizzle hadn't seen us.

We went back to work.

"The next step is to mix all the ingredients together," said Carlos.

Once again, the bus helped us. As it beat the batter, it forced in air.

Ralphie reminded us that cooks and chemists are really alike.

"They both measure out ingredients," he said. "And mix them together to make something new. The only difference is that cooks get to taste what they make."

So it *is* a matter of taste.

Let's hear it for taste tests.

The baker was looking for us again. We had to do something quickly.

"Submarine doowwwnn!" yelled Carlos.

With that, the bus dove into the batter.

When the baker saw the bowl of batter, he was surprised. "When did I make this?" he wondered. "I must be going do-nuts!"

He poured the batter into a pan and put it in the oven. Things began to heat up.

"Why is it getting so hot?" cried Wanda.

"I am pleased to announce," said Carlos, "the addition of the last ingredient—HEAT!"

Ralphie gasped. "Carlos?"

"Yes!" said Carlos. "We're in the oven!"

That meant one thing—we were about to become dessert!

How did she know we were *in* the oven?

Just when we started to panic, Ralphie pointed to a funny figure moving through the batter. Liz opened the bus door and the Friz came in.

"Phew!" she said. "It feels like somebody forgot to put up the heat shield."

Quickly, Liz pressed a button and the shield went up. The temperature dropped.

"As I always say," said the Friz, "if you can't stand the heat, get out of the oven."

"Look!" yelled Phoebe. "The batter's moving."

Dorothy Ann explained, "According to my research, the baking soda is making bubbles."

"The batter's not the only thing getting pushed around," pointed out Arnold.

He was right. The bus was also moving. We could hear a strange noise, too.

"It's steam!" said Carlos.

The Friz didn't seem worried. "It's so hot that the water in the batter is becoming vapor," she said. "It's making bubbles."

Wanda noticed something else. "The batter is starting to look kind of solid," she said.

And so it was. The cake was done.

"Oh, no!" exclaimed Arnold. "We're going to have our cake and be eaten, too!"

Things did look bad. Ms. Frizzle tried some levers on the bus, but nothing worked.

"We're doomed!" cried Arnold.

This takes the cake!

"Wait! I've got an idea," said Dorothy Ann. "Do we have any baking soda and vinegar left?"

Luckily, we did.

"You see," said Dorothy Ann, "baking soda plus vinegar equals . . ."

Carlos finished for her. ". . . the gas pressure we need to push us out of here."

They were right. Carlos put a balloon over the end of the container. Then he and Dorothy Ann put it on the back of the bus. The rest of us put on our seat belts.

When the baker took the cake out of the oven, the bus flew out of the cake. The baker chased us, but we got away through the mail slot.

Back at school, things were normal again. Well, as normal as they ever are with Ms. Frizzle. We had a great party, and she really seemed surprised. At least, she was very pleased. When she asked, "Class, where did you get such a lovely cake?" we giggled.

Carlos explained, "The baker just gave it to us . . . said it was ruined . . . something about a moth."

Ms. Frizzle laughed and said, "Chemistry is a piece of cake." She was right!

Boy: Is this the bakery that the Magic School Bus visited?

Baker: Yes, yes it is.

Boy: Mmmm. Those donuts look good. I'll bet you a donut I can tell you something really important that was left out of the book.

Baker: Impossible!

Boy: It was . . .

Baker: Was it that Dorothy Ann is a little young to be doing those experiments?

Boy: Not really. Ms. Frizzle was there. Everyone knows you need a grown-up when you do chemistry experiments. And Dorothy Ann was wearing goggles.

Baker: I'll bet you two donuts that some people think chemicals are bad for them.

Boy: No, some chemicals are good. It depends on what you use them for.

Baker: Okay, three donuts that maybe you think that things like salt and sugar don't really look like building blocks and diamonds.

Boy: They do under a microscope.

Baker: You're bluffing. I'll bet you all my donuts that you can't tell me what was missing.

Boy: You never said how old Ms. Frizzle is!

Baker: Upon my pastry! You're right about that!

From the desk of Ms. Frizzle
An Experiment for Parents, Teachers, and Kids

Dorothy Ann showed you what happens when baking soda and vinegar are mixed together. What happens if something else is added? Try this to find out.

1. Fill a pitcher with water.

2. Add three teaspoons of white vinegar and two teaspoons of baking soda.

3. Drop in five or six salted peanuts. Watch what happens.

Here's why. The vinegar and baking soda make a chemical reaction and cause bubbles (made of carbon dioxide). Bubbles tend to gather on surfaces, so they cling to the peanuts. Since peanuts are light, the bubbles lift them up to the top of the pitcher. At the top, the bubbles break and in a while the peanuts sink again. At the bottom, the peanuts gather more bubbles and up they go.